MISS GENEVA'S LANTERN

MISS GENEVA'S LANTERN

by Mary Dixon Lake

illustrated by Mary Frances Robinson

For Aunt Ophelia, Auntie Rose, and Uncle Mark—M.D.L.

To Rodney Roddel—M.F.R.

Text copyright © 1997 by Mary Dixon Lake
Illustrations copyright © 1997 by Mary Frances Robinson

For information contact:
MONDO Publishing
One Plaza Road
Greenvale, New York 11548

Designed by Edward Miller
Production by Our House

Printed in Hong Kong by South China Printing Co. (1988) Ltd.
99 00 01   9 8 7 6 5 4 3

ISBN 1-57255-228-X

A Note About the Story

People born and raised in the American South love to tell stories. Some stories are so old, no one really knows where they first came from. Others arise from unexplained occurrences encountered in the rural part of town. This is one of the stories I heard my mother tell. To this day, I believe it is a true story.

—*M.D.L.*

Inez Garvey lived in Middleville, Georgia, with her mama and papa. They had enough land to have a two-horse farm. In the 1940s, a two-horse farm in Middleville was pretty good, indeed.

Inez knew her way all around Middleville, on the roads and in the woods. Papa had taught her about the woods. He would take Inez with him when he went looking for the herbs, roots, and special plants used for medicine and cooking. Inez knew which plants to touch and which ones not to touch.

Inez started out on the dusty, red clay road. Miss Darcy lived just up the road a-ways, but it was almost evening, and Inez didn't want to be out on the road after dark.

Not that she was afraid. But to tell the truth, the only thing Inez did not like was going by the two strange houses. One was midway between her house and Miss Darcy's. It was empty now because old Mr. Boone had passed on about two years ago. Some folks said that since then they've seen him sitting on his front porch, rocking in that old rocker, just a-smiling and a-waving like always.

But Inez had never seen Mr. Boone, and she knew this was just old folks' talk.

The other house was closer to Inez's house and could actually be seen from her porch. It sat up on a hill and had a big green barn beside it. Miss Geneva lived there. Inez had never seen her up close. Hear tell she was a widow-woman who did not talk much to anybody. She never went to town and she hardly ever left her house, except to check on her chickens. Every night, rain or shine, she'd take a walk to her barn, her lantern bobbing up and down as she went.

Inez walked along the road in the late afternoon heat.
Then she ran like the wind past the two strange houses,
never turning her head once to look. She didn't slow
down 'til she reached Miss Darcy's.

"Good evening, child," said Miss Darcy. "Isn't your mama
sweet! Here, bring her some of my grapes in return," she said.

"Thank you, ma'am," said Inez, breathing in the sweet grape
smell. "Mama surely will make some good jelly out of these."

Inez hopped off Miss Darcy's porch and set out for home.

"Be sure to thank your mama for me, Inez," Miss Darcy called after her.

"Yes, ma'am," Inez called back as she waved goodbye. "And thank you!"

Inez walked along the dusty road. The shadows started to lengthen as she made her way back home.

Maybe I have time to dig up an elephant-ear lily for Mama, thought Inez. She had seen one the other day when she was out with Papa. How beautiful it would be growing right under the kitchen window. Mama could see it every time she looked out.

The sun was just beginning to set. Inez figured she could dash into the woods, dig up an elephant-ear, and be back home in time for supper.

Inez skipped along the road, humming, until she reached the woods.

After her eyes adjusted to the leafy darkness, Inez followed the path she had taken with Papa. Soon she saw the elephant-ear, and she dug it up with a stick. *Mama will be pleased,* Inez thought as she headed home.

The sun seemed to be hiding now, and Inez walked faster
to beat the dark. Just as she reached old Mr. Boone's house
she heard a noise. CREAK, CREAK, CREAK, CREAK, CREAK. Inez
tried not to look. *Maybe it's the door,* she thought, *or an open
window.* CREAK, CREAK, CREAK. At last, she couldn't help
herself. She turned her head, and in the hazy dusk Inez saw
a man sitting in the old rocker on Mr. Boone's porch, moving
back and forth, back and forth, back and forth, creaking,
creaking, creaking.

And the next thing she knew, Inez found herself running so fast her feet barely touched the ground. Beads of sweat ran down her face as she ran faster and faster. It was dark now, and Inez could hardly see the road. She never even saw the small hole in the path. But then she fell.

As she tried to get up, Inez felt someone grab her arm. She closed her eyes and tried to scream, but nothing came out.

Then she heard a woman's voice.

"Can I help you, child?" Inez looked up and saw a smiling face above her, all aglow. She could not say why, but she was not afraid.

"Yes, ma'am, thank you," Inez said, taking a deep breath. She stood up slowly. A gray-haired woman was standing in front of her, holding a lantern.

"What are you doing out here alone in the dark?"

"I was trying to get this. . . oh no, oh no!" cried Inez.

"Calm yourself, child. What is it?" coaxed the woman.

"The elephant-ear lily. I lost it. It was for Mama!"

"Is that all?" said the woman with the lantern. "Well then, maybe I can help you."

"But, I have to get home," said Inez. "It's almost supper time."

"Never you mind. I will see that you get home right quick," the woman assured her.

The gray-haired woman with the lantern walked arm in arm with Inez. Soon they were in front of Miss Geneva's house.

"This is where I live," the woman said. "I have a few elephant-ears around back. I will gladly give you one for your mama if you will dig it up yourself."

"You will?" said Inez.

"I sure will."

"Are you Miss Geneva?" Inez asked.

"One and the same," responded the woman.

Inez felt numb. She could hardly speak. "But I thought you were like a witch. I heard you were the meanest of the meanies!" she blurted out.

Miss Geneva laughed and laughed.

"Yes, I know the stories people tell," she said, shaking her head. "Do you think I'm like a witch now?"

"Why, no, I surely don't. But I saw Mr. Boone. That's why I was so scared, and ran so fast, and lost Mama's lily," Inez said.

"Come with me, child," said Miss Geneva, holding out her free hand.

Miss Geneva showed Inez the elephant-ears she owned, and she pointed to one Inez could dig up for Mama.

As Inez dug up the plant, Miss Geneva talked. "You know, you needn't be afraid of old Boone. 'Haints never bother good people and children. I know you were afraid, but don't be," Miss Geneva explained.

Miss Geneva walked Inez down the hill to the beginning of her yard. Then Inez heard her mother call, "Nez, come to supper."

"Good night, now, " Miss Geneva said. "You run along home."

"Good night, Miss Geneva. And thank you," Inez called as Miss Geneva disappeared down the road, her lantern bobbing up and down.

"Mama, Mama," Inez yelled as she burst into the kitchen. "Look what I got for you!"

Mama smiled her biggest smile. "My, my, my. What a lovely elephant-ear. Where did you get such a fine one?"

Inez smiled and kissed her mama on the cheek. Then Mama put the lily in some water and set it on the windowsill.

The next day, Mama planted the elephant-ear lily right under the kitchen window. Inez could tell Mama really liked it.

At dinner that night, Papa said, "Have y'all heard about the widow-woman up the road?"

"Heard what?" Mama asked.

"Hear tell she up and passed on all of a sudden this morning."

Inez looked up. "You mean Miss Geneva?" she asked.

"That's right. Seems she was on her way to the barn, probably to check on her chickens," Papa explained.

Later that night, Inez could not sleep. She climbed out of bed and went out on the porch. The stars in the sky seemed to be twinkling brighter than usual. As she looked up the hill towards Miss Geneva's house, Inez saw a light flicker and bob. It looked like a lantern going around and around the old green barn. Inez stood there, watching the light slowly circle the barn again and again. Then it disappeared into the darkness. Inez remembered Miss Geneva's words. She turned, went into the house, and climbed back into bed.

The next day, on her way home from school, Inez walked past Mr. Boone's house and up the hill to Miss Geneva's. She slipped a card she had made under the front door of the house.